Milly and Molly

For my grandchildren
Thomas, Harry, Ella and Madeleine

Milly, Molly and Oink

Copyright© Milly Molly Books, 2003

Gill Pittar and Cris Morrell assert the moral right to
be recognized as the author and illustrator of this work.

Published by
Milly Molly Books
P O Box 539
Gisborne, New Zealand
email: books@millymolly.com

Printed by Rhythm Consolidated Berhad, Malaysia

ISBN: 1-86972-002-4

10   9   8   7   6   5   4   3   2   1

Milly, Molly
and
Oink

"We may look different
but we feel the same."

No barnyard is complete without a pig.
In fact Farmer Hegarty had two pigs,
Rosie and Rascal.

Every year Rosie would build herself a nest
in the dry grass and have nine little piglets.
They were round and fat and some of them
were spotty, just like Rascal.

But, this year was different. Instead of
having nine little piglets, Rosie had ten.
The tenth little piglet was tiny.

But what he lacked in size, he made up for in noise. The tenth little piglet never stopped 'oinking'.

Because he did not have the size and
strength to push between the other piglets
to get his meals, he grew thinner and
thinner. The littlest piglet was fading away
and so was his 'oink'.

Farmer Hegarty decided to put him in a
pen of his own and asked Milly and Molly
to look after him.

Milly and Molly were delighted. They named
the little piglet Oink. They bathed him
regularly with a cake of soap.

They fed him all their left-overs, stirred
up in warm milk.

One day Milly and Molly decided Oink
was ready to eat his meals from a trough,
just like the big piglets did.

They taught Oink to push a box up to
the trough and climb onto it, so he could
reach his meals.

Oink began to thrive and he loved
to chat with everyone.
"Oink must be careful," warned Farmer
Hegarty. "If he strays onto the road a bad
stranger could make friends with him
and then we might never see him again."

Sure enough, one day Oink had gone.
Milly and Molly called and called.
Every day they kept his water fresh...
just in case he returned.

Meanwhile, Oink had been stuffed into
the trunk of a car.

He was thrown into a pen with a big
fat greedy pig.
Again Oink grew thinner and thinner.

One day the thief threw a box of cabbages
into the pen. This time Oink wasn't upset
that the big fat greedy pig did not share.
Oink was more interested in the box.

He waited until all the cabbages had
been eaten and it was dark. Then he
pushed the box with his nose until it was
under the gate latch.

He climbed onto the box, just like Milly
and Molly had taught him and slipped
the latch undone.

He opened the gate just enough to squeeze
through. Then he ran for his life.

Oink did not get far before he came to a
fence. He could hear the farm dogs barking
and he saw the thief's lights go on.

He quickly rolled onto his side
and squeezed and squeezed.

Once Oink was through the fence he did not
look back. And when he reached the road
to home, he slowed down to a trot.

When Milly and Molly went to Oink's pen
the next morning to freshen his water...
they couldn't believe their eyes!
There he was, waiting for his meal.

Once again Oink began to thrive.
But, forever after, he was very wary
of strangers.

Milly, Molly and Oink

The value implicitly expressed in this story is 'beware of strangers' - be cautious of people you don't know.

Milly and Molly learn through Oink's mistake to be wary of strangers.

"We may look different but we feel the same".

B O O K S

Other picture books in the Milly, Molly series include:

- Milly, Molly and Jimmy's Seeds   ISBN 1-86972-000-8
- Milly, Molly and Beefy   ISBN 1-86972-006-7
- Milly, Molly and Taffy Bogle   ISBN 1-86972-001-6
- Milly, Molly and Betelgeuse   ISBN 1-86972-005-9
- Milly and Molly Go Camping   ISBN 1-86972-003-2
- Milly, Molly and Pet Day   ISBN 1-86972-004-0